Grandpa's Boneshaker Bicycle

written and illustrated by
Colin West

PICTURE WINDOW BOOKS
Minneapolis, Minnesota

Editor: Nick Healy
Page Production: Brandie E. Shoemaker
Creative Director: Keith Griffin
Editorial Director: Carol Jones

First American edition published in 2007 by
Picture Window Books
5115 Excelsior Boulevard
Suite 232
Minneapolis, MN 55416
877-845-8392
www.picturewindowbooks.com

First published in 1999 by A&C Black Publishers Limited, 38 Soho Square,
London W1D 3HB, with the title GRANDAD'S BONESHAKER
BICYCLE.

Printed in the United States of America.

Library of Congress Cataloging-in-Publication Data
West, Colin.
Grandpa's boneshaker bicycle / by Colin West. — 1st American ed.
p. cm. — (Read-it! chapter books)
Summary: Grandpa, a collector of fine junk, trades his antique
"turn-of-the-century rear-driven safety bicycle" for a modern mountain bike.
ISBN-13: 978-1-4048-2732-5 (hardcover)
ISBN-10: 1-4048-2732-3 (hardcover)
[1. Grandfathers—Fiction. 2. Bicycles and bicycling—Fiction.] I. Title.
II. Series.
PZ7.W51744Gr 2006
[Fic]—dc22   2006003581

Table of Contents

Chapter One

This is a story about my grandpa.
He lives in an amazing house in the
middle of town.

It is easy to spot Grandpa's house.
It is the one with all the statues and
garden gnomes outside.

And inside, Grandpa's house is full
of junk. From top to bottom, it is
crammed with fascinating things.

Grandpa has collected useless objects
for as long as he can remember. He
never throws anything away.

Even Grandpa's garden shed is full of junk. One day, during my summer vacation, I was snooping around. I came across a rusty old bicycle.

"Bless me!" said Grandpa. "If it isn't my old boneshaker bicycle!"

"How old is it?" I asked.

"Well, let's see," said Grandpa. "I bought it more than 50 years ago, and it was secondhand then."

"Let's get it going again," I said.

"Yes, I would," said Grandpa.

"Yes, it is," said Grandpa.

So we dusted it down and cleaned it up. We patched the inner tubes and pumped up the tires.

We polished up the seat and washed down the fenders. We checked the brakes and oiled the wheels.

At last it was ready to try out.
Grandpa was a bit wobbly at first.

And sure enough, Grandpa soon got the hang of it again.

Grandpa was so pleased with his bike that we decided to go on a ride the next day.

Chapter Two

The following day, I met Grandpa.
We rode to the edge of town.

After a while, Grandpa began to
fall behind. I could see that he was
getting pretty tired.

"Should we go back now?" I asked.

"Not on your life!" said Grandpa, who sounded out of breath. "Look at that sign over there."

Today at Clover Park: Rummage SALE! Turn left ahead.

Grandpa can never resist the thought of buying more useless objects, so we cycled on.

Luckily, the ride was downhill all the way to Clover Park. We left our bikes and started looking around.

Almost immediately, Grandpa saw something he liked.

Grandpa paid the lady 50 cents for the clock, and we moved on. As we headed for the next table, we noticed someone fiddling with Grandpa's bike.

The stranger was taken by surprise.

"I thought this old bicycle was for sale," he explained.

"Well, it's not," said Grandpa.

"Oh, that's a shame," sighed the man.

Grandpa shook his head.

The man thought for a moment.

"How about $100?" he asked.

Grandpa was a little surprised, but
he shook his head. The man thought
for another moment.

I whistled. Two hundred and fifty
dollars is a lot of money.

But Grandpa still refused.

"Oh, well," said the stranger. "If you change your mind, please get in touch. My name's Mr. Bell, by the way." He said goodbye and gave Grandpa his card.

Mr. Bell's
CYCLE MUSEUM
& Shop
Buy a NEW bike!
Repairs undertaken
See the Antique Cycles!

"He must be crazy to offer me all that money for my old boneshaker bike," said Grandpa.

Secretly, I thought Grandpa must be crazy to turn down the offer.

We put the clock in Grandpa's saddlebag and left for home.

The ride back was hard work for Grandpa. "I'm not sure biking is such a good idea," he said as we reached his house.

I helped Grandpa off his bike, and
we went inside.

Grandpa put the clock on the mantel
and tucked the card from Mr. Bell
behind it.

We put our feet up and sipped our lemonade. After a while, I said, "I'll visit again tomorrow." But Grandpa seemed lost in thought. I wasn't sure if he heard me.

Chapter Three

The next day, Grandpa greeted
me with a huge grin. "Hello," he
said. "We're going on another
bicycle ride."

"Where are we going?" I asked.

"Just follow my directions," Grandpa said as we set off.

After half an hour, I had no clue
where we were.

But then I spotted a sign, and it all
became clear.

We parked our bikes and went inside.

The museum was marvelous. I had never seen so many bicycles.

There were bikes and trikes of every size, shape, color, and age.

As Grandpa admired a modern racing bike, I noticed someone outside on an old high-wheeler. I looked again and saw it was Mr. Bell.

Chapter Four

After a while, Mr. Bell came inside.
He recognized us right away. "Well, if
it's not my friends from the rummage
sale!" he exclaimed.

"I hope you're enjoying my museum. It's the finest in the land," Mr. Bell said proudly. But then he looked sad. "There is a space here, though," he sighed. He pointed to an empty stand.

We just don't have a turn-of-the-century rear-driven safety bicycle.

"Is that what mine is?" asked
Grandpa. When Mr. Bell nodded,
Grandpa cleared his throat.

"Another bike?" asked Mr. Bell,
looking interested.

Grandpa explained.

Mr. Bell began to brighten up.

He happily led us to his shop at the
back of the museum.

There were rows and rows of new bicycles in the shop.

"I bet you would like a bike for doing your shopping," Mr. Bell said.

"Not really," said Grandpa.

Mr. Bell looked rather surprised, and I was quite surprised myself.

Chapter Five

Mr. Bell wheeled out the coolest mountain bike I had ever seen. "This is our top-of-the-line model," he said. "It has 15 gears, and it's fit for a world champion."

Grandpa climbed on. The bike seemed just the right size for him.

Mr. Bell opened the door. "Why don't you try it outside?" he said.

47

After a good test ride, Grandpa said he would love to swap his old bike for the new one.

We all shook hands and said our goodbyes.

We cycled home the long way. We
went through the park,

over the trail,

and along the riverbank.

And this time, I had a hard time keeping up with *Grandpa*!

Look for More *Read-it!* Chapter Books

Looking for a specific title? A complete list
of *Read-it!* Chapter Books is available on our Web site:
www.picturewindowbooks.com